This book belongs to
my friend:

_____

A NOTE TO PARENTS

Fear of the unknown is a common emotion, especially among young children. It is not unusual, for instance, for children to be afraid of the dark. In *Nighttime Noises,* Little Bill has trouble falling asleep because of his overactive imagination.

In this story, Little Bill is kept awake by several noises he has trouble identifying. To show your child that the noises in the story are nothing to be afraid of, encourage him to guess the source of each. As Little Bill seeks out family members for advice, discuss each person's method of handling fear. Talk about what you and your child can do when you are afraid of the dark or when something else frightens you. Stress that each person develops different ways of dealing with fear.

If your child experiences bedtime frights, work with him to make his bedroom a place he feels comfortable in, even at night. In good weather, try spending time outside before bed. Look at the stars, listen to the wind, and talk about nocturnal insects and animals. Show your child how comfortable *you* are in the dark. Bring a flashlight, read *Nighttime Noises,* and remind your child that although Little Bill feels scared sometimes, like your child, he is always safely surrounded by those who love him.

Learning Fundamental: 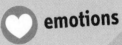 emotions

For more parent and kid-friendly activities, go to www.nickjr.com.

Nighttime Noises

Published by Scholastic Inc., 90 Old Sherman Turnpike, Danbury, CT 06816

SCHOLASTIC and associated logos are trademarks and/or registered trademarks of Scholastic Inc.

ISBN 0-7172-6626-5

Printed in the U.S.A.

First Scholastic Printing, November 2002

Nighttime Noises

by

Samantha Berger

illustrated by

Dan Kanemoto

SCHOLASTIC INC.

New York Toronto London Auckland Sydney
Mexico City New Delhi Hong Kong Buenos Aires

"*Chugga chugga, chugga, chugga, choo choo!* All aboard the Little Bill Express!" Little Bill called, as he chugged into his room.

"Next stop . . . BED!" said his father.

"Can I stay up just a little longer?"
Little Bill asked.
"Sorry, baby. It's time for the
caboose to get some rest in the
station," his mother said.

"Goodnight, Little Bill," said his mother.

"Goodnight, son. We love you," his father said.

"I love you, too," said Little Bill. "Don't forget to leave the lamp on until I fall asleep, and don't forget to say goodnight to Captain Brainstorm and Elephant!"

"Goodnight Captain Brainstorm," his mother said to Little Bill's favorite toy.

"Goodnight Elephant," his father whispered to Little Bill's pet hamster.

Little Bill lay in bed and watched Elephant curl up into a little ball. "I wish I could fall asleep that quickly," he thought to himself.

He pulled up his quilt. Then suddenly he heard something. *Ka-thump!* The sound was coming from the closet.

"Mama?" said Little Bill. "MAMAAA!" he called even louder.

Little Bill's mother poked her head into the room.

"Mama, I'm scared. I think I heard a monster in the closet," Little Bill told her.

"Well, let's investigate together," she replied.

Little Bill's mother opened the closet door. A baseball
rolled out. "Could this be your monster?" she asked.
Little Bill giggled. "I guess so."

"When I feel afraid," said his mother, gently squeezing his hand, "I check the facts. Once I know everything's all right, I'm not scared anymore."

"I feel better already," Little Bill said. "Thanks, Mama. Goodnight."

Little Bill closed his eyes. But in only a few seconds, he heard another sound. *Scratch, scratch, scraaatch.* This time, the sound was coming from outside his window.

He walked to the window to investigate, but the sound got louder and louder. He turned and ran into his brother's room.

"I think there's a dragon climbing outside my window.
I'm scared," Little Bill gasped.

"Don't worry, Little Bill," said his sister, April. "It's
probably just the wind."

"When I used to get scared," his brother, Bobby, said, "I'd listen to music or read a book to take my mind off of it. Why don't you try that?"

Little Bill took a deep breath. "Okay, Bobby. I'll try."

April took Little Bill's hand. "I'll tuck you in," she told him.

April gave Little Bill a book and kissed him goodnight. He had barely finished looking at the first page when he heard a new noise. *Clank, clank, clank.* This time, it was coming from the wall. Little Bill put his ear to the wall and heard it again. "Uh-oh," he thought and ran out of the room.

Little Bill found his great-grandmother, Alice the Great, having a cup of tea. "Goodness, Little Bill! Are you still awake?" she asked.

"I'm scared," explained Little Bill. "It sounds like a big troll is banging on my walls!"

Alice the Great smiled. "You know, Little Bill, when the heat comes on it makes a banging noise. I'm sure that's what you heard."

Alice the Great put her arm around Little Bill. "Do you know what I do when I feel frightened? I say a special little rhyme, and it seems to do the trick!"

Alice the Great continued:

"*Listen, thing that's scaring me,*
Go away when I count to three—
One . . . two . . . three!
It works every time. Why don't you try it?"

"I will," Little Bill said, giving his great-grandmother a kiss.

Alice the Great tucked Little Bill in under his special quilt. But as soon as she left, Little Bill heard something else. *Crash!* This time, it sounded like it was right under his bed! Little Bill wondered if it was a big, huge, gigantic giant. He tried to remember what everyone had told him to do if he got scared.

First he looked around, just like his mother.
He didn't see anything. Next he tried reading his
book, just like Bobby suggested. That didn't work
either, so he tried Alice the Great's special rhyme.
"Listen, thing that's scaring me,
Go away when I count to three—
One . . . two . . . three!"
But when he got to three, he was still afraid.

Suddenly Little Bill
thought of someone else
who might be frightened.
"Elephant, are you scared,
too?" he asked.

Elephant stood on his
back legs and wiggled his
little nose.

"Don't worry, Elephant!"
said Little Bill. "I'll take
care of you!"

Little Bill wrapped his quilt around his shoulders, closed his eyes, and took a deep breath. "Listen, giant," he shouted. "This is *my* room and *my* pet. Nobody's allowed to scare Elephant, so go away right now!"

He opened his eyes, kneeled down, and lifted the bedcovers to face the giant. "Go away . . . " he started to say again. But then he laughed. There wasn't a giant under his bed after all!

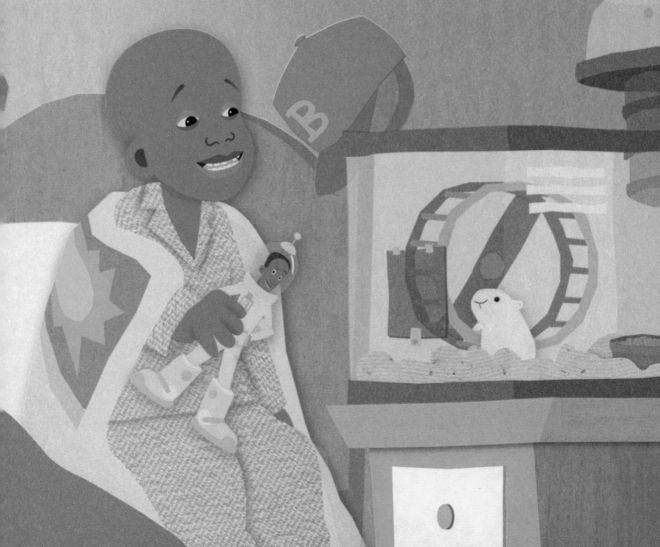

"Captain Brainstorm!" Little Bill cried. "You fell off the bed!" He turned to Elephant. "Don't worry, Elephant, you're safe now. You can always count on me when you're afraid."

Little Bill tickled Elephant. Then he crawled back into bed with Captain Brainstorm. A moment later, all three of them were fast asleep.